little Miss Fickle

by Roger Hargreaves

Would you like me to tell you a story?

If you were Little Miss Fickle,
you'd say, "Yes, please!"
And then you'd say, "No, thank you!"
And then you'd say, "Yes!" again.

Little Miss Fickle was one of those people
who just could not make up their minds.

Ever!

About anything!

Little Miss Fickle lived in Dandelion Cottage
which was on the outskirts of Sunnytown.

And she lived right next door to her best friend,
Little Miss Neat, who lived in Twopin Cottage.

One Monday, Little Miss Fickle and
Little Miss Neat went out to lunch in Sunnytown.

"I'll have the soup to start with," said
Little Miss Neat to the waiter as she looked
at the menu, "followed by the fish."

"So will I," said Little Miss Fickle.

But after the waiter had written down the order,
Little Miss Fickle looked at the menu again.

"No I won't," she said. "I'll have the salad instead,
followed by the roast chicken!"

The waiter crossed out the first order, and
wrote down the second.

"On the other hand," continued Little Miss Fickle,
"I won't have anything to start with...
but then I'll have the eggs!"

The waiter sighed.

An hour later, after the waiter had worn out three pencils and four order pads, Little Miss Fickle finally made up her mind to have the soup, followed by the fish.

The waiter brought the soup.

Little Miss Fickle looked at it.
"I'm not hungry any more," she said.

It was at that moment that the waiter decided he was going to be a bus conductor instead of a waiter.

On Tuesday, Little Miss Fickle went to
buy a hat.

"I want a new pink hat," she announced to
the milliner.

The milliner brought her two pink hats
to choose from.

"I'll have this one," said Little Miss Fickle, after
she had tried them both on.

"Certainly, Madam," replied the milliner,
and put the hat in a hatbox.

"On the other hand," said Little Miss Fickle, "I think I'll have the other hat!"

The milliner took the first hat out of the hatbox... and then put the second hat into the hatbox!

"But," continued Little Miss Fickle, "I think the first hat suited me better, don't you?"

The milliner didn't say a word as she took the second hat out of the hatbox... and then put the first hat back into the hatbox!

She handed the hatbox to Little Miss Fickle.

Little Miss Fickle looked at the milliner.

"Do you have any blue hats?" she asked.

It was at that moment that the milliner decided she was going to be a ballerina instead of a milliner!

On Wednesday, Little Miss Fickle went to the butcher's.

"I'd like some sausages," she said.

"Beef sausages, or pork sausages?" asked the butcher.

"Pork sausages," replied Little Miss Fickle.

The butcher wrapped up the pork sausages.

"But beef sausages would be nicer," said
Little Miss Fickle.

The butcher unwrapped the pork sausages,
and wrapped up some beef sausages instead.

"On the other hand," continued Little Miss Fickle,
"chops would be tastier!"

It was at that moment that the butcher
decided he needed a holiday.

But, on Thursday, guess what happened?
Little Miss Fickle disappeared!
Little Miss Neat had seen her pass Twopin Cottage
on the way into Sunnytown, but she hadn't come back.

She didn't come back on Friday, either.
So Little Miss Neat went looking for her.

She met Mr Muddle.
"Have you seen Little Miss Fickle?" she
asked anxiously.
Mr Muddle looked at her in a puzzled sort of a way.
"Did you say, 'Have I been for a little tickle?' " he asked.
"Oh, Mr Muddle," said Little Miss Neat, and hurried on.

Then Little Miss Neat met Mr Forgetful.

"Have you seen Little Miss Fickle?" she asked.
Mr Forgetful thought.

"Well," she said, "have you?"
Mr Forgetful thought again.

"Have I what?" he asked, after a while.
"Oh, Mr Forgetful," said Little Miss Neat,
and hurried on.

But could she find Little Miss Fickle?
No, she could not!
Nobody had seen her.

The Sunnytown Public Lending Library has...
nineteen thousand,
nine hundred,
and ninety-nine books.

On Saturday afternoon, Little Miss Fickle reached up
and took one of them down from a shelf.

"I'll read this one," she thought to herself.

"On the other hand," she thought again, looking at
another book, "perhaps I'll read that book instead!"

She put the first book back on the shelf,
and took the other book down.

It was the nineteen thousand,
nine hundred,
and ninety-ninth book she had chosen!

Little Miss Fickle had been in the library for three
days choosing a book.

Three whole days choosing just one single,
solitary book!

She went home carrying her book.

That Saturday afternoon, Little Miss Neat was in the garden of Twopin Cottage when Little Miss Fickle walked past.

"Where have you BEEN?" she called out.

"To the library," replied Little Miss Fickle.

"For THREE days?" exclaimed Little Miss Neat.

"Well," explained Little Miss Fickle,
"I wanted to choose the right book!"

And she held it up.
And then she stopped and looked at it.

"Oh, botherations!" she said.
"I've read it before!"

3 Great Offers for MR. MEN Fans!

MR. MEN TOKEN

1 New Mr. Men or Little Miss Library Bus Presentation Cases

A brand new stronger, roomier school bus library box, with sturdy carrying handle and stay-closed fasteners.

The full colour, wipe-clean boxes make a great home for your full collection.

They're just £5.99 inc P&P and free bookmark!

☐ MR. MEN   ☐ LITTLE MISS (please tick and order overleaf)

2 Door Hangers and Posters

In every Mr. Men and Little Miss book like this one, you will find a special token. Collect 6 tokens and we will send you a brilliant Mr. Men or Little Miss poster and a Mr. Men or Little Miss double sided full colour bedroom door hanger of your choice. Simply tick your choice in the list and tape a 50p coin for your two items to this page.

PLEASE STICK YOUR 50P COIN HERE

Door Hangers (please tick)
☐ Mr. Nosey & Mr. Muddle
☐ Mr. Slow & Mr. Busy
☐ Mr. Messy & Mr. Quiet
☐ Mr. Perfect & Mr. Forgetful
☐ Little Miss Fun & Little Miss Late
☐ Little Miss Helpful & Little Miss Tidy
☐ Little Miss Busy & Little Miss Brainy
☐ Little Miss Star & Little Miss Fun

Posters (please tick)
☐ MR.MEN
☐ LITTLE MISS

CUT ALONG DOTTED LINE AND RETURN THIS WHOLE PAGE

3 Sixteen Beautiful Fridge Magnets – any **2** for **£2.00!** inc.P&P

They're very special collector's items!
Simply tick your first and second* choices from the list below
of any 2 characters!

1st Choice

☐ Mr. Happy
☐ Mr. Lazy
☐ Mr. Topsy-Turvy
☐ Mr. Bounce
☐ Mr. Bump
☐ Mr. Small
☐ Mr. Snow
☐ Mr. Wrong

☐ Mr. Daydream
☐ Mr. Tickle
☐ Mr. Greedy
☐ Mr. Funny
☐ Little Miss Giggles
☐ Little Miss Splendid
☐ Little Miss Naughty
☐ Little Miss Sunshine

2nd Choice

☐ Mr. Happy
☐ Mr. Lazy
☐ Mr. Topsy-Turvy
☐ Mr. Bounce
☐ Mr. Bump
☐ Mr. Small
☐ Mr. Snow
☐ Mr. Wrong

☐ Mr. Daydream
☐ Mr. Tickle
☐ Mr. Greedy
☐ Mr. Funny
☐ Little Miss Giggles
☐ Little Miss Splendid
☐ Little Miss Naughty
☐ Little Miss Sunshine

*Only in case your first choice is out of stock.

--- **TO BE COMPLETED BY AN ADULT** ---

**To apply for any of these great offers, ask an adult to complete the coupon below and send it with
the appropriate payment and tokens, if needed, to MR. MEN CLASSIC OFFER, PO BOX 715, HORSHAM RH12 5WG**

☐ Please send ____ Mr. Men Library case(s) and/or ____ Little Miss Library case(s) at £5.99 each inc P&P

☐ Please send a poster and door hanger as selected overleaf. I enclose six tokens plus a 50p coin for P&P

☐ Please send me ____ pair(s) of Mr. Men/Little Miss fridge magnets, as selected above at £2.00 inc P&P

Fan's Name _____

Address _____

_____ **Postcode** _____

Date of Birth _____

Name of Parent/Guardian _____

Total amount enclosed £ _____

☐ **I enclose a cheque/postal order payable to Egmont Books Limited**

☐ **Please charge my MasterCard/Visa/Amex/Switch or Delta account** (delete as appropriate)

Card Number

Expiry date ___ / ___   **Signature** _____

MR.MEN   **LITTLE MISS**
Mr. Men and Little Miss™ & ©Mrs. Roger Hargreaves

CUT ALONG DOTTED LINE AND RETURN THIS WHOLE PAGE